Karen's Brothers

Little Sister

Karen's Brothers

Ann M. Martin

Illustrations by Susan Tang

A
LITTLE APPLE
PAPERBACK

SCHOLASTIC INC.
New York Toronto London Auckland Sydney

ISBN 0-590-43643-0

12 11 10 9 8 7 6 5 4   1 2 3 4 5 6/9

Printed in the U.S.A.   40

First Scholastic printing, April 1991

*This book is for
my goddaughter,
Rachel Andrea Eichhorn,
born July 2, 1990.*

Welcome, Rachel Ann

Karen's Brothers

Karen and Ricky

"Gotcha!"

"No, you didn't."

"Did too. Now you're It!"

Ricky Torres and his friend Bobby Gianelli were fooling around in our classroom. They were playing Kleenex tag, which you can play with almost anything. If you play with a paper towel, then the game is called towel tag. If you play with an eraser, then it is called eraser tag.

Kleenex tag is very easy to play. All you need is some Kleenex. Instead of tag-

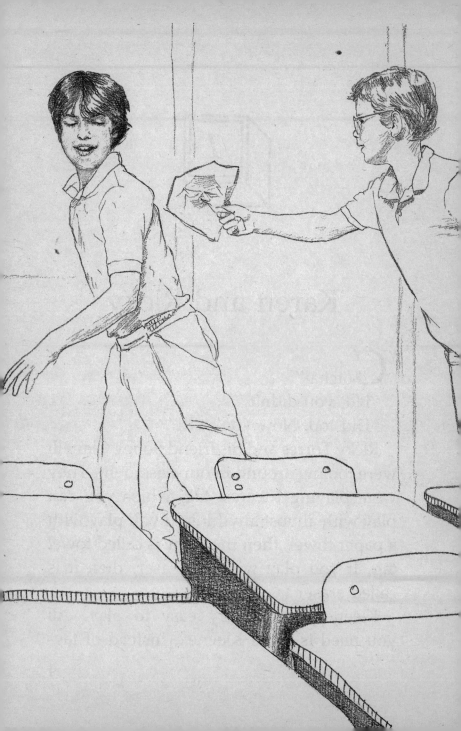

ging someone with your hand, you tag him (or her) with a piece of the Kleenex. The problem is that you can't always *feel* a Kleenex tag. Which is why Bobby said that Ricky had not tagged him.

"Do over!" called Bobby.

"No. I'm not going after you again," said Ricky. "I already got you."

"Did not."

"Did too."

Bobby leaned over a desk and swiped at Ricky's arm with his Kleenex. "Okay. Now *I* got *you*, so you *have* to get me back!"

Ricky ran after Bobby. Both of them ran into a desk.

CRASH!

It was a good thing that our teacher, Ms. Colman, had not arrived yet.

I looked at my best friends. We rolled our eyes. Boys are *so* silly. I can say that even though I am married to Ricky. He might be my pretend husband, but he is still a boy.

I have two best friends — Nancy Dawes and Hannie Papadakis. Nancy lives next door to Mommy's house. Hannie lives across the street (sort of) from Daddy's house. Nancy and Hannie and I call ourselves the Three Musketeers. We are very glad that we are all in the same second-grade class at Stoneybrook Academy.

I am glad Ricky is in my class, too. (Well, usually I am glad.) Ricky and I and another girl, Natalie Springer, sit in the front row because we wear glasses. I sit next to Ricky, which is good. But Hannie and Nancy get to sit in the back row.

There are some people in my class that I do not like. One of them is Pamela Harding. She thinks she's so great. Two others are Pamela's friends, Leslie and Jannie. They think they are so great, too.

I am not sure how I feel about Bobby Gianelli these days. I used to like him okay. Even if he is a bully. I liked him a lot when he was in the wedding that Ricky and I held on the playground. He wore a suit to school and everything. Still, I was a little cross. It seemed that lately Ricky was spending more time with Bobby than he was with me. I guess that was not Bobby's fault.

Then I thought of something. Maybe it was *my* fault. Maybe Ricky felt I spent too much time with Hannie and Nancy. Or maybe I had done something wrong. Maybe I had done something to make Ricky angry.

But what? What could make him mad at his very own wife?

I looked at Ricky. He and Bobby had stood up. They had straightened the desk they had fallen over. (And they had checked the hallway to make sure Ms. Colman wasn't coming.)

Now Ricky stuffed the Kleenex in one of his pockets. He pulled an eraser from another pocket. "Eraser tag!" he shouted.

Ricky had not even said hi to me that morning. Was he too busy? Had he not noticed me? Or was he angry?

I sat down at my desk to think.

2

Two and Two
and Two . . .

I knew that Ms. Colman would arrive in about five minutes. So I had five minutes of thinking time.

I began by thinking about Ricky and feeling bad. But I couldn't feel *too* bad. After all, it was a going-to-Daddy's Friday. Most kids like Fridays anyway. But I like every other Friday the best of all. That's because of going to Daddy's house. My little brother, Andrew, and I get to spend the weekend at our daddy's big house here in Stoneybrook, Connecticut.

Who am I? Oh. I guess I forgot to tell you. Well, I'll take care of that now. I am Karen Brewer, and I am seven years old. Andrew is almost five years old. We both have blond hair and blue eyes. I have freckles, too. And I wear glasses all of the time. Not just for reading.

Mostly, Andrew and I live at the little house with Mommy. But every other weekend, and on some holidays, plus two weeks in the summer, we live with Daddy. Why do Mommy and Daddy have two different houses? Because they are divorced. Mommy and Daddy used to be married. But that was a long time ago. It was when they had Andrew and me. After that, they decided they did not love each other anymore. They loved Andrew and me, but not each other. So Mommy left the big house, where we had all been living. (The big house belongs to Daddy's family. Daddy grew up there.) Mommy found a little house, and she and Andrew and I moved into it. Daddy stayed in his house. And then . . . Mommy and

Daddy each got married again.

So Andrew and I have two houses and two families. At the little house are Mommy and Seth (he's our stepfather), and Rocky and Midgie. They are Seth's cat and dog. My rat lives at the little house, too. Her name is Emily Junior. Andrew and I live at the little house most of the time.

At the big house live Daddy and Elizabeth (she's our stepmother) and a lot of other people, plus some animals. Four of the other people are Elizabeth's kids. Sam and Charlie are so old they go to high school. David Michael is seven, like me, but a few months older. (He *never* lets me forget that.) Sam, Charlie, and David Michael are my stepbrothers. My stepsister is Kristy. She is thirteen. She baby-sits. She is one of my all-time favorite people. At the big house, I also have an adopted sister. Her name is Emily Michelle. (Emily Junior is named after her.) Emily Michelle is two years old. Daddy and Elizabeth adopted her. She comes from

Vietnam, which is very far away. Another person at the big house is Nannie. Nannie is Elizabeth's mother, so she is my step-grandmother. Nannie takes care of Emily while Daddy and Elizabeth are at work. And of course Andrew and I live at the big house sometimes.

These are the pets at Daddy's: Boo-Boo, Shannon, Goldfishie, and Crystal Light the Second. Boo-Boo is Daddy's big, fat, mean cat. Shannon is David Michael's puppy. Goldfishie is Andrew's goldfish, and Crystal Light the Second is my goldfish. (Crystal Light the First died. I gave her a gigundo nice funeral.)

Since Andrew and I go back and forth between Mommy's house and Daddy's house so much, we have two of lots of things, one at Mommy's and one at Daddy's. I have two bicycles, one at the big house, one at the little house. I have two stuffed cats. Moosie stays at the big house, Goosie stays at the little house. Plus, I have clothes and toys and books at each house. That is why I sometimes call myself Karen Two-Two. (I call my brother Andrew Two-Two.) The name came from the title of a book Ms. Colman read to our class. The book was *Jacob Two-Two Meets the Hooded Fang*.

Mostly, I like being a two-two. I like having two houses and two mommies and two daddies and two best friends. But I do not have two of *every*thing. For instance, I do not have two Ticklys. (Well, I do now, but I did not used to.) Tickly is my special blanket. There was only one Tickly at first. And I kept forgetting and leaving him behind at one house or the other. Finally, I had to tear Tickly in half so I could have a piece at each house. I did not like doing that. Plus, I do not have two of Kristy or Sam or Charlie or David Michael or Emily or Crystal Light the Second. I miss them when I am at the little house. And when I am at the big house, I miss my rat.

Uh-oh. I had gotten way off the subject. I had not thought about Ricky at all. And now Ms. Colman had arrived.

Maybe I could talk to Ricky on the playground that day.

Just a Girl

All morning I thought about what I might have done to make Ricky mad at me. I did not pay much attention to Ms. Colman. Once, she had to say, "Karen?" three times before I heard her.

"Yes?" I replied.

"Could you please answer the question?"

"What question?" I asked.

Everyone laughed. Well, Nancy and Hannie did not laugh. But a lot of other kids did. Pamela and Jannie and Leslie laughed the loudest. (Ricky only laughed a little. But

12

I did not think my own husband should have laughed at all.)

By recess time, I still did not know what I could have done to make Ricky mad at me. I decided, though, that I should make up with him. I would be very nice to him. Then maybe I could say, "Ricky, I'm sorry for what I did. Whatever it was." And then Ricky would pay attention to me again.

Hannie and Nancy and I stood together on the playground.

"Let's play hopscotch," said Nancy.

"No, jump rope," said Hannie.

"Hopscotch."

"Jump rope."

"Karen? What do you want to do?" asked Nancy.

"What?" I replied. I was gazing across the playground. I was watching Ricky. He and Bobby were tossing a football around.

"Hopscotch or jump rope?" Nancy said impatiently.

"I don't know. . . . Look at Ricky over there."

"Karen is not paying attention," Hannie said to Nancy. "She will not be able to keep her mind on anything. So I guess we can't jump rope. We need three people for that."

"Yea! Hopscotch!" cried Nancy.

Hannie and Nancy pulled their hopscotch stones out of their pockets.

" 'Bye," I said to them. "I'm going to talk to Ricky."

I ran across the playground to where Ricky and Bobby were playing football. I watched them for a few minutes. Then I called, "Hey, Ricky! Hey, Bobby!"

Ricky caught the ball that was sailing toward him. Then he said, "Yeah?"

I tried to sound very friendly. "You know what?" I began. "My brothers play football all the time. Sometimes I play with them."

Ricky and Bobby looked at each other. Then Ricky said, "Yeah?" again.

"So can I play with *you?* I would really like to."

Ricky did not answer at first. He looked

like he was thinking very hard. At last he said, "Nah. You're just a girl."

"*So?*" I yelled.

"Why are you shouting?" asked Ricky.

"Because you called me a girl!"

"Well, you *are* a girl."

"But that doesn't mean I can't play football."

"Girls don't play football!" shouted Bobby.

"*I* do!" I shouted back.

Ricky looked as if he were getting mad. "Not with us!" he cried. He tossed the football to Bobby.

I stamped my foot. "I'm not talking to you anymore, Yicky Ricky Torres."

"Good!" he replied. (I do not think he meant it.)

I turned my back on Ricky.

Then I stomped away.

Just a Boy

Was I ever glad to go to the big house. I needed something to make me feel better. And a weekend at the big house usually makes me feel very good. Don't worry. I like the little house. I like Mommy and Seth. But things are usually more exciting at Daddy's. There are so many people and animals around.

I just love noise and excitement. (Andrew does not.)

The weekend at Daddy's started off fine. On Friday night, we had strawberry ice cream for dessert. Then Kristy let me dress up in her clothes. And on Saturday morning, a bunch of Sam and Charlie's friends came over.

That was when something went wrong with the weekend.

The big kids — Sam and Charlie and their three friends — were sitting in the living room. They were trying to decide what to do. They let David Michael and me sit around with them.

David Michael and I like the big kids. For one thing, Charlie can drive. His car is called the Junk Bucket. Driving is very important because you can go anywhere you want. If I want to go to a store or to a movie, I have to ask an adult to take me. But Charlie can just drive off in his car.

For another thing, the big kids are gigundo fun.

"So what are we going to do?" asked Charlie. He was sitting on the floor. He was all sprawled out. He was eating potato chips, even though we had just finished

breakfast. (Daddy says that Charlie must have a hollow leg.)

"Nintendo?" suggested John Hastings.

"If I play another game of Nintendo, my brain will fry," said Sam.

"Go over to Mouth's?" said Charlie. (Mouth is another big kid. I am not sure what his real name is.)

"Mouth and his family are away for the weekend," replied John.

"How about a movie?" asked Sam.

All the big kids seemed to like the idea. I glanced at David Michael. He was smiling. I smiled back. We *love* the movies.

After about a million hours, the boys decided what movie they wanted to see. It was a space adventure!

"Charlie?" spoke up David Michael. "Can you lend me four dollars?"

"What for?" asked Charlie.

"The movie. I don't have enough money."

Before Charlie could answer, I said, *"I'll* lend you the money, David Michael. I've got enough for both of us." (I had been saving my allowance for a very long time.)

"Wait a sec!" exclaimed Sam. "You guys aren't coming with us."

"Oh, o-*kay*," said David Michael angrily.

But I did not give up so easily. "Puh-*lease* — " I began.

"Karen," Sam interrupted, "you wouldn't understand the movie. You're — "

"I know, I know. I'm just a girl!" I cried.

I do not think Sam or Charlie or their friends heard me. John and Charlie had already left the house. Sam and the others were putting on their jackets. They were heading out the door. As soon as they had stepped onto the porch, I slammed the door behind them.

"Karen, you don't have to be *so* mad," said David Michael. "They wouldn't let me come, either."

"Oh, what do *you* know?" I cried. "You're just a *boy*."

"I can't help it," said David Michael. He was smiling. He thought that was funny.

I knew better.

5

A Is for Awful

I stomped off. It seemed like I was always stomping away from boys.

I stomped up the stairs, along the hall, and into my bedroom.

I slammed my door shut.

"BOYS ARE AWFUL!" I shouted to Moosie and Tickly. "You know what's so bad about them?"

I picked up Moosie and made him shake his head.

"You don't know?" I asked. "Okay. I will tell you. I bet I can think of something bad about them for every letter of the alphabet. I will even write them down." I sat at the table in my big-house room. With a red crayon I wrote on the top of a piece of paper: BOYS. Underneath that, I wrote: A is for Awful, B is for Barf-breath, C is for Crazy, D is for Dumbbells . . .

I went right down the list. I had a little trouble with X, but finally I wrote: X is for X-tra Mean.

"Okay, Moosie? You see? This is how bad boys are. Well, not all of them, I guess. They are not *all* crazy, and they do not *all* have barf-breath. But, as a group . . . *they* ARE *AWFUL!*"

I read my list a few times. Then I thought of something. Ricky is a boy. (Duh.) I had told Ricky that I would not speak to him. Now I had found out that all boys were awful. So I decided not to speak to *any* of them. I would not talk to Daddy or Seth. I would not talk to David Michael or Andrew or Sam or Charlie. I would not even speak to Boo-Boo, Midgie, or Goldfishie. (They are boy pets.) And I especially would not talk to Ricky or Bobby — or to any other boy in my class. It was a good thing that my best friends are girls. And it was good that Ms. Colman is a girl. I did not know how I could get through a day at school without talking to my friends or my teacher.

All that day I would talk only to Elizabeth, Nannie, Kristy, Emily Michelle, and Shannon. At first my brothers and Daddy kept saying, "What's wrong?"

I did not answer them.

Then, at dinnertime, David Michael said, "I think Karen is mad at us."

"At who?" asked Andrew.

"Us boys."

"Me, too?" said Daddy. "I haven't done anything."

I leaned over to Kristy. I whispered, "I'm not speaking to *any* boys. They are all jerks. Tell them I said that."

Kristy said, "Karen wants everyone to know that she's not speaking to boys because they are all jerks."

"What are you going to do at Christmas?" Sam wanted to know. "How are you going to sit on Santa's lap and tell him what you want?"

I leaned over to Kristy and whispered again. Then Kristy said, "Karen says she'll write Santa a letter."

"Oh," said Sam.

When I got back to the little house on Sunday, I was still not speaking to Andrew. And I would not speak to Seth or Midgie, either.

"Karen," said Mommy, "I think you are hurting the boys' feelings."

"Well, they hurt mine."

Mommy did not say anything. But later I heard her tell Seth, "Don't worry. I'm sure Karen will just forget about all this."

Oh, no, I won't, I thought.

24

6

The We Hate Boys Club

The next morning, Mrs. Dawes drove Nancy and me to school. When I left the little house to go over to Nancy's, I called, "Good-bye, Mommy! Good-bye, Emily Junior! Good-bye, Rocky!"

When we reached school, Mrs. Dawes let us out by the front walk. She watched Nancy and me until we were safely inside the building.

Guess what Nancy and I saw when we entered Ms. Colman's room. We saw Bobby and Ricky playing lip tag.

It was a new game.

Ricky had invented it.

Lip tag is a kind of Kleenex tag. You have to tag the person on the lips with a piece of Kleenex. At least, that was what Hannie thought. Hannie had gotten to school early. She had been watching Ricky and Bobby.

Nancy and I watched them, too. The three of us stood in a back corner of our classroom. While we watched, Bobby ran away from Ricky and the Kleenex. He ran by someone's desk and tripped over a pair of boots. When he landed on the floor, Ricky tackled him.

"Gotcha!" he cried. He fluttered the Kleenex over Bobby's lips.

I looked at Hannie and Nancy. "Boys . . . are . . . dumb," I announced. I told them what had happened at the big house on Saturday.

Just as I was finishing my story, something sailed across the room. It hit Hannie on the head.

"Ow!" she exclaimed.

She had been hit by a paper airplane.

26

Bobby and Ricky were finished playing lip tag. Now they were folding paper airplanes. Somebody's aim was not too good.

"Sorry!" yelled Ricky.

"That's okay," replied Hannie. But she did not look like she meant it. The next thing she said was, "Do you know what Linny did yesterday?" (Linny is Hannie's older brother.) "He went through my best Bobbsey Twins book. He drew glasses on all the girls, and mustaches on all the boys. He used *ink*. He thought he was being so cool and funny."

"You know what?" I said suddenly.

"What?" asked Hannie and Nancy.

"We should start a boy-hating club. We could call it the We Hate Boys Club."

"Yeah!" exclaimed Hannie.

"Okay," said Nancy. "No boy has done anything mean to me. But if you guys are going to start a club, I want to be in it."

"Good," I replied.

I had been speaking loudly.

Pamela and Jannie and Leslie were standing nearby. I knew they had heard what I said. And I did not care.

"What will the We Hate Boys Club do?" Nancy wondered.

"We will not talk to *any* boys," I replied at once. "Not even to our fathers or boy pets. I am already not talking to boys. That is because Ricky and my brothers are awful, crazy dumbbells with barf-breath."

"But I'm not mad at my daddy," said Hannie. "Or at Noodle the Poodle."

"I'm not mad at my daddy, either," said Nancy.

"Okay. We will change the rules," I said. "How about if we don't talk to any boys in school, but outside of school you can do whatever you want?"

"Great," replied Hannie.

"Fine," said Nancy. "I just hope we don't get sent to the principal's office. The principal is a boy. How could we not talk to him?"

"Don't worry about it," said Hannie. She crumpled up the paper airplane and threw it at Bobby.

7

The We ♥ Boys Club

Once, Linny Papadakis told Hannie that a long time ago, Indians lived where Stoneybrook is now. Ever since, Hannie and Nancy and I have spent about one recess period each week looking for arrowheads. We dig around in the dirt. We have not found any arrowheads. But we will not give up.

We had been searching for arrowheads for about ten minutes on the day we formed the We Hate Boys Club, when suddenly I stood up.

"Yuck! Gross!" I exclaimed. "Look at my

hands. It's too muddy to dig for arrowheads today. I'm going to the girls' room to wash up."

"I think I'll stay here," said Nancy. "I feel lucky today."

"Me, too," said Hannie.

So I went to the girls' room by myself. There are only two stalls in the bathroom. Both of the doors were shut. That was okay. I just had to wash my hands. All I needed was the sink, some towels, and a lot of soap.

I turned on the water. I was rubbing soap onto my hands when I heard a voice behind me say, "Leslie?" It was Pamela! Leslie and Pamela were in the stalls. And they didn't know I was in the bathroom. I decided to eavesdrop until the toilets flushed.

"Yeah?" Leslie replied.

"Did you hear about the We Hate Boys Club?"

"That thing Karen Brewer was talking about this morning?" said Leslie. "Yeah. I did. It is *so* lame."

"Plus, Karen has a big mouth. She

31

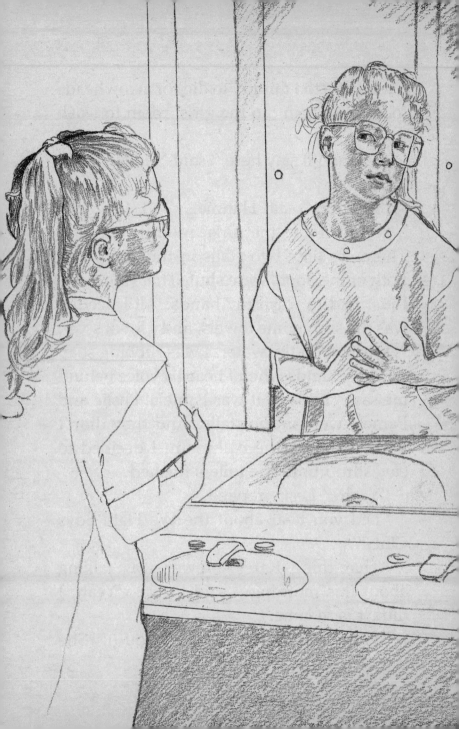

wouldn't be able to stop talking to *any*one. Not even boys."

"Besides, the boys are just going to get more mad at the stupid Three Musketeers," said Leslie in a singsong voice. "The We Hate Boys Club isn't going to help at all."

"Well, I have an idea," said Pamela.

"Oh, goody!" (Leslie likes *all* of Pamela's ideas.)

"We should start," Pamela said, "the We Love Boys Club. Only we'll draw a heart instead of writing the word *love*. And then we'll call our club the We Heart Boys Club. That sounds good. It's sort of like 'we hate boys,' only it is much, much nicer."

"Cool!" exclaimed Leslie. "I'm sure Jannie will want to join. What will our club do?"

"First we'll just watch Karen and Nancy and Hannie. We'll see what they do. Then we'll try to make the boys feel better. When the other girls won't talk to them, *we* will. And when — " Pamela suddenly stopped speaking. "Ooh, I just thought of something!" she cried. "If Karen and Ricky aren't speaking to each other, and Ricky and I *are,* then maybe Ricky will divorce Karen — "

"And marry me!" squealed Leslie.

"No, *me,*" said Pamela.

"Oh. Okay."

I could not believe it. Had Pamela just said that she wanted Ricky to marry *her?* Had she really said that? What a gigundo stupid-head!

I dried my hands quickly. Then I left the girls' room. At Stoneybrook Academy, you are not supposed to run in the halls. But I did anyway. I ran all the way outside. I ran to Hannie and Nancy. (They had not found any arrowheads.)

"You guys!" I cried. "Guess what."

"What?" said Hannie.

"What's wrong?" asked Nancy. She looked worried.

"Pamela and Jannie and Leslie are going to start a club against ours! They are going to call it the We Heart Boys Club. And

Pamela is going to try to steal Ricky from me." I told my friends everything I had overheard.

We were so mad that we were madder than *gigundo* mad.

8

Buttons and Banners

The We ♥ Boys Club was pretty bad. In fact, it was so bad that the members of the We Hate Boys Club could not think of anything worse. But when Hannie and Nancy and I got to school the next day — guess what. We found something that really was worse.

Pamela and Leslie and Jannie were already in our classroom. They were dressed alike. And they were wearing buttons that looked like this:

"Oooh," said Nancy softly.

My friends and I glanced at each other.

"They actually formed a club," said Hannie.

"And they *look* like it," added Nancy. "Anybody could tell they are in a very special club. They look like they belong together. But nobody would know that *we* belong together, too."

I looked at our clothes. Nancy was wearing a blue plaid dress. (It was new.) Hannie was wearing a yellow sweater and a yellow-and-red skirt. I was wearing my unicorn sweat shirt and blue jeans.

I narrowed my eyes at Pamela. (She did not see me.) How dare Pamela make her club better than ours? The We Hate Boys Club did not seem like a club at all. Boo.

But did I say that to Hannie and Nancy?

No. I did not want them to know what I was thinking. Instead I said, "You know, everyone is going to make fun of the We Heart Boys Club. Everyone will laugh at Leslie and Jannie and Pamela. You'll see." I stared at our enemies.

"Why will everyone laugh at them?" Hannie wanted to know.

"Because they are saying they *love boys.* Dumb old boys."

"Oh, yeah," said Hannie.

"We might as well pick a fight," I went on. "You guys do what I do."

I stepped closer to the We ♥ Boys Club. I began to sing, *"Pamela li-ikes boys! Pamela li-ikes boys!"*

Hannie and Nancy joined right in. So did Natalie and the twins.

But Pamela and her friends did not seem upset.

Neither did Ricky. In fact, he looked pleased. And he certainly did not make fun of Pamela.

When Nancy, Hannie, Natalie, and the

twins and I stopped singing, Ricky said, "I'm glad *some*body likes us." Then he gave me a Look.

Uh-oh. I guessed that Look was because I was not speaking to him.

"Okay. So not everyone hates boys," I said to Nancy and Hannie. "But *we* do. And we have good reasons."

"Yeah," said Hannie and Nancy.

"But you know what?" I went on. "I think we have some work to do. We should seem more like a club."

"How about making buttons of our own?" suggested Nancy.

"That would just be copying," replied Hannie.

"Posters? Banners?" I said.

"Nah. The boys would rip them down," Nancy pointed out.

"Oh, brother. We have to do *some*thing," I said. "Let's work on this at recess. Okay, you guys?"

"Okay," replied Nancy and Hannie as Ms. Colman came into the room.

9

"We Hate You Boys and Always Will"

At recess on Tuesday, Hannie and Nancy and I did not jump rope. We did not play hopscotch. We did not look for arrowheads.

What *did* we do? We held a club meeting. We stood in a corner of the playground as far away from everybody as we could get.

"I had an idea this morning," I announced.

"Goody. I was hoping you would," said Hannie. "You always get such good ideas. What did you think of?"

"A club song," I answered.

"Great! How does it go?"

"Well, I didn't write it yet. I was hoping that you and Nancy could help me. It would be fun to write a song together."

"A club song," repeated Nancy thoughtfully. Nancy just loves to sing and dance. She wants to be an actress one day. (I would not mind being an actress myself.) "Let's see," Nancy went on. "I think the song should start out with something about hating boys."

"We hate you boys!" cried Hannie.

"And always will," I added.

"We hate you boys, you're such big pills!" sang Nancy.

"That is a very good beginning," I said proudly.

When we finished our song, this is how it went:

We hate you boys, and always will.
We hate you boys. You're such big pills.
It doesn't matter if you're Ricky or Bill.
We hate you boys, and always will!

"Next," I said, "we need a secret boy-hating sign. It will be our club symbol." I knelt on the ground. I found a stick. Then I stopped. I frowned.

"Draw a circle," Nancy suggested.

So I did. That gave me a great idea. This would be our sign:

"One last thing," I said. "How about a hand signal?"

"I know one!" Hannie exclaimed. "Watch." She held her index fingers in front of her and crossed them. They made an X.

"Perfect!" I cried. "Okay, let's sing our song."

Nancy and Hannie and I sang "We Hate You Boys" at the tops of our lungs. But no one heard us. That was because everyone in the second grade was watching the boys play football. My friends and I ran over to

our classmates. We sang our song again.

But guess what? Pamela and Leslie and Jannie began screaming at the tops of *their* lungs. They cheered, "Two, four, six, eight. Who do we appreciate? Boys, boys, YEA!" Then they smirked at Hannie and Nancy and me.

My friends and I sang our song again. Even *more* loudly.

The members of the We ♥ Boys Club cheered their cheer again.

So I shouted, "Woo-woo! You *love boys!*"

And Pamela shouted, "Stupid-head, dumbbell, you hate your own husband!"

And Nancy shouted, "You guys think you are *so* cool!"

And Pamela shouted, "In case you haven't noticed, we are *not* guys."

And Ricky shouted, "Would you girls shut up? I can't concentrate."

But the bell rang then. Recess was over. Ricky would not need to concentrate on his football game after all.

Pamela's Note

Maybe Ricky was mad at Pamela during the football game. But he was not mad at her after the game. I know because I heard Pamela say to him later, "Ricky, please don't be mad at Leslie and Jannie and me. We didn't mean to bother your game."

And Ricky answered, "That's okay, Pamela." He smiled at her. She smiled back.

"Gross," I said to Nancy and Hannie.

* * *

The next day, my friends and I got to our classroom early. In huge letters, we wrote on the chalkboard: BOYS ARE STUPID.

Ricky saw the message as soon as he got to our room. He picked up an eraser. He wiped away BOYS. In its place he wrote: GIRLS. Now the message read: GIRLS ARE STUPID.

I frowned. Hmm . . .

Just then Pamela came into the room. She saw the message. She saw Ricky holding a piece of chalk. She said, "Ricky, you don't really think *all* girls are stupid, do you?"

Ricky looked worried. "No," he said. So he wrote MOST in front of GIRLS. The new message read: MOST GIRLS ARE STUPID.

Under that Pamela wrote: ESPESHIALLY KAREN, HANNIE, NANCY.

"You can't even spell!" I cried. I erased KAREN, HANNIE, NANCY, and wrote: PAMELA, THE STUPIDEST OF ALL.

While we were busy at the board, Natalie Springer had been hanging around the door to our room. Suddenly she whispered loudly, "Here comes Ms. Colman!"

By the time Ms. Colman reached our room, the board was clean. And we were sitting quietly at our desks.

On Thursday I left a package in Ricky's desk. It was small and wrapped in tin foil. I put a note on top. The note said: From the We ♥ Boys Club.

When Ricky opened the package, he found a hunk of mud inside.

To prove that she had not made the mud brownie, Pamela brought Ricky a whole boxful of real, chocolate brownies the next day.

"Gee, thanks!" exclaimed Ricky.

"Oh, gross," I muttered.

At the little house, Seth and Andrew tried to trick me into talking to them. Once, we were watching TV after dinner. Andrew pointed to the wall over my head. His eyes grew very round. "Uh-oh," he said.

And Seth added, "Karen, watch out! There's a big spider!"

They knew that I knew they were tricking me. They expected me to say crossly, "There is *not* any old spider!" But I kept my mouth shut. I just stared at the TV.

Seth and Andrew shrugged at each other.

On Friday, another bad thing happened.

We were writing in our math workbooks. Ms. Colman was busy in the back of the room. I heard someone whisper, *"Pssst! Ricky!"*

Ricky turned around in his seat. "What?" he whispered. He sounded annoyed.

I looked over my shoulder. I looked just in time to see Pamela pass a note to Ricky. Ricky unfolded it quietly. While he read it, I remembered something. I remembered Pamela talking to Leslie in the bathroom. She had said that maybe Ricky would marry *her*.

Oh, boy. Did this note mean that Pamela and Ricky liked each other? Would Pamela marry Ricky now?

My stomach began to feel funny. Maybe the We Hate Boys Club had not been such a good idea. What had I done?

Ricky finished reading the note. He turned around again. He and Pamela grinned at each other.

Oh, no. Oh, no-o-o-o-o.

Football

I was back at the big house. Two weeks had gone by since Charlie and Sam had said I could not go to the movies with them. So I had not spoken to my brothers or my daddies (or Midgie or Boo-Boo or Goldfishie) for two weeks.

The night before, when Andrew and I had arrived at the big house, everyone was there to greet us.

"Hi, Kristy! Hi, Emily! Hi, Elizabeth! Hi, Nannie! Hi, Shannon!" I cried. I kissed them.

50

"What about us *guys?*" asked Charlie.

I turned to Kristy. "Tell *him*," I said, "that I am a member of the We Hate Boys Club. I do not talk to boys."

"I'm not deaf," Charlie said to Kristy. "I heard that."

"Good," replied Kristy. "Because I'm getting tired of talking for Karen."

"Yeah, you're just being silly, Karen," added David Michael.

"How long are you going to keep this up?" Elizabeth asked me.

"As long as I have to," I answered.

"Well, I hope you don't need anything from your father or from one of your brothers," said Kristy.

"What if I do? I'll just ask you to ask for it."

"Maybe I won't do that," replied Kristy. "And maybe my mom won't do it, either. And maybe neither will Nannie."

"I'll ask Emily Michelle then," I said.

"Try asking her to say something right now." Kristy was challenging me.

51

"Okay. Emily?" I said. Emily looked up at me. "Tell Daddy I want my allowance."

"No," said Emily.

"Say, 'Daddy, Karen wants her allowance.' "

"No," said Emily again.

"See? It's the Terrible Twos," Kristy told me wisely. "Emily says no to practically everything these days. Your only hope is to teach Shannon to talk."

I scowled. "Hmphh," I said.

On Saturday, the big kids came over again. Three friends of Charlie and Sam. This time the boys did not hang around trying to decide what to do. They already knew what they wanted to do.

"Play football," said Sam.

I was spying on the boys from the front hallway. I groaned. Football again.

The next thing I knew, the boys were putting on their coats. Sam left to find the football. I sat on the bottom of the stairs and watched the big kids. David Michael sat down next to me and watched them, too. (I moved as far away from David Michael as I could get. I did not even look at him.)

"Hey, Karen, David Michael. Want to play football with us?" asked Charlie.

"Me?" David Michael said.

"*Me?*" I squeaked. (Uh-oh, I had just spoken to a boy.)

"Sure," replied Charlie. "You guys are great players."

David Michael and I jumped up. We dashed outside after the big kids. In a few minutes, I was running around with my brothers and their friends. We had a gigundo fun time! We did not play a real game, but that was okay.

"Good catch, Karen!" Charlie yelled.

"Thanks," I replied. "Hey, David Michael, I'm going to tackle you!"

We fooled around all morning. Then we got hungry. We ate lunch together in the kitchen. I talked a mile a minute.

Nobody said anything about this, though.

Karen's Great Idea

After the football game, things changed. I felt better. My brothers had asked me to *play* with them. It did not seem to matter that I was a girl.

I decided to see what happened if I talked to Daddy. I found him putting on his coat. He was holding his car keys.

"Where are you going?" I asked.

"To the hardware store," he replied.

"Can I come?"

"I don't think it will be much fun."

"Okay. I'll come anyway."

So Daddy and I got into the car. We drove downtown. I told Daddy about school. I told him that Nancy might start taking dancing lessons. We had a very nice talk. I expected Daddy to say, "Karen, I am glad you are speaking to me again." But he did not.

When Daddy and I got home, I looked for Andrew. Andrew was busy crashing cars around the playroom.

"Hi," I said. "Can I play, too?"

"Okay," Andrew replied.

We crashed cars together. Then we built a block highway for the cars. Later that day I talked to Boo-Boo. I even talked to Goldfishie. By Sunday evening, everything seemed back to normal. It was nice not to hate boys anymore. But something seemed wrong. Nobody — not one boy — had asked why I was talking to him again. Did the boys even care?

Then I thought of something. I had not apologized to anyone. And I owed *lots* of apologies. I owed apologies to all of my brothers, to Daddy, to Seth, to Boo-Boo, to Midgie, and to Goldfishie.

And to Ricky Torres.

I had been pretty mean to them. But I am not always very good at saying "I'm sorry." And I was not good at all at saying so many "I'm sorries." Besides, I *had* had a reason for being angry and hating boys. How could I apologize to everyone without getting a lot of rude comments back?

I thought about this while I waited for Mommy to pick up Andrew and me.

I thought about it while Mommy drove us to the little house.

I thought about it during dinner that night.

And at last I got a great idea!

13

Brother's Day

What was my great idea?

It was Brother's Day!

There is a Father's Day. There is a Mother's Day. There is even a Grandparents' Day. Why couldn't there be a Brother's Day?

If there were a Brother's Day, I could have a party for the boys I had been mean to. Maybe the boys were not all *my* brothers, but they were all *some*body's brother. Even the pets. Midgie had been born in a big litter of puppies. Some of them were boys. Boo-Boo had had four brothers and sisters. (Daddy told me so once.) I did not know for sure if Goldfishie had a brother, but I decided that he probably did.

Okay. I would give the boys a Brother's Day party. A party would be my way of saying "I'm sorry." Plus, maybe I could really say "I'm sorry" at the party. Nobody would make rude comments at a party that was especially for them . . . would they?

I did not think so. Not if the party were gigundo fun and nice. And I wanted it to be that way. After all, I did not *truly* hate my brothers or my daddies or Ricky or Midgie or Goldfishie or Boo-Boo.

What would we do at a Brother's Day party? I wondered.

Anything I wanted! I was making up Brother's Day, so I could invent Brother's Day parties, too. Let's see. I would serve yummy food. Maybe we would play games. I could make presents for the guests. Cards, too. And I could make a big apology speech to the boys.

I wondered if Ricky would come to the party. I knew my brothers would. I was not mad at them anymore. But all Ricky knew was that I had thought up the We Hate Boys Club. I had not started talking to him yet.

Then I wondered about something else. Would Seth come to the party? I would probably have the party at the big house in two weeks. That would make sense. All of my brothers, one of my fathers, and two of the pets would be there. But would Seth feel comfortable at the big house? If he brought Midgie, would Midgie get along with Boo-Boo?

Oh, well. I could not worry about those things now. First, I had to know just who would be at the party. And the only way to do that was to send out invitations and see who could come.

I sat down with a stack of paper and some

crayons. "Hmm," I said. "Let's see." I thought for a moment. Then I wrote:

A NEW HOLIDAY
COME TO MY BROTHER'S DAY PARTY!
ARE YOU MY BROTHER?
DO YOU HAVE A BROTHER?
THEN THIS PARTY IS FOR YOU!

I wrote that the party would be at the big house in the playroom. (That was the only way Goldfishie could be at the party. His tank is in the playroom. His equipment is plugged into the wall there.) Then I wrote that we would play games and pig out. I wrote that the human guests would get presents. (I did not think I needed to make presents for the boy animals. But maybe I would make cards for them.)

Suddenly I had a lot to do. I had to mail the invitations. I had to think up presents.

I had to *make* the presents. I had to make cards for everyone. I had to decide what kind of food to serve.

But before I did anything else, I had to call Daddy and Elizabeth. I had to ask for permission to have a Brother's Day party in two weeks.

Chocolate Chippies

Daddy and Elizabeth liked the idea of a Brother's Day party. They said it was okay to have it in the playroom at the big house. Then Daddy added, "Just be sure that you clean up any messes you make."

"Okay," I said. (How come parents are always thinking about messes?)

That was on Monday.

On Tuesday morning I mailed my invitations.

On Tuesday afternoon I began making

Brother's Day cards. I had to make ten of them. That did not matter. I like to make things. I used Magic Markers and lots of glitter to make the cards. Each one was different. Each one was also big. The cards were so big that I could not find envelopes for them. Finally, I had to make the envelopes, too.

When the cards were finished, I thought about presents. What could I make? It is always so hard to make gifts for boys.

Then I remembered the pile of empty coffee cans in the basement of the little house. Mommy uses them for lots of things. So does Seth. But I bet that they would not mind giving seven of them to me.

I was right.

Once I had the coffee cans, I began to work hard on seven different boy presents. There would be one each for Andrew, my stepbrothers, Daddy, Seth, and Ricky.

When I had made the gifts and wrapped them up, I telephoned Nannie at the big house. "Nannie?" I said. "You know the Brother's Day party I am giving?"

"Yes," said Nannie.

"Well, I was wondering if you could help me with the refreshments." (I remembered to add "please.") "I would like to serve punch and chocolate chip cookies."

"Chocolate chippies?" asked Andrew. He was standing right behind me. He was listening to me talk on the phone.

"*Shhh*, yes," I said to Andrew.

"Goody!" he exclaimed.

So on the Thursday before Brother's Day, I went to the big house after school. Nannie helped me to bake lots of chocolate chippies. We also baked one batch of cookies without chocolate in them. That is because David Michael cannot eat chocolate. (Poor thing. I *love* chocolate gigundoly.)

While I was getting ready for my party, I decided something. I decided that my friends and I would have to stop the We

Hate Boys Club. We would have to break it up. So one day I said to Hannie and Nancy, "I don't think we need our club anymore."

"Good," replied Nancy. "Because I am still not mad at any boys."

"And I am *tired* of being mad at boys," said Hannie.

Nancy and Hannie and I started talking to the boys again.

But Pamela and Jannie and Leslie did not stop wearing their "I ♥ Boys" buttons. They were as nice as nice could be to all the boys. Maybe that was why the boys did not seem to notice that my friends and I were talking to them after all. They were too busy listening to the girls in the We ♥ Boys Club. The girls kept telling the boys how great the boys were and bringing them cookies.

Ricky gave me funny looks when I talked to him now. He never said much back to me. I guess he was pretty mad. So he *had* to come to my Brother's Day party. He just had to. That way, I could show him that I still liked him.

But Ricky did not mention anything about my party.

Finally I had to say to him, "I hope you got my invitation. Are you coming to the party?"

Ricky shrugged. "I guess so," he replied.

15

Ready or Not

At last Friday arrived. It was a going-to-Daddy's Friday. It was also the day before Brother's Day. I was all ready for my party.

On Thursday, Nannie and I had baked the chocolate chippies. And the plain cookies for David Michael. When the cookies had cooled, I put them in a box. It was not just any old box. It was a special Brother's Day box. It was big and it was made of white cardboard. I had decorated it using crayons. On the top, I had written HAPPY BROTHER'S DAY! On the sides I had drawn stars and flowers and sailboats. I was very proud of the box. I was sorry I had to leave it at the big house.

As soon as I got home from school on Friday, I said, "Mommy? Can Andrew and I go to Daddy's early today? Like right now?"

Mommy looked up from the book she was reading. "Sorry, sweetie," she said. "The agreement is that you and Andrew don't go until dinnertime."

"Boo. I want to check on things for my Brother's Day party."

"You've got an awful lot of things to check on right here," Mommy pointed out.

That was true. Seven coffee-can gifts were at the little house. So were ten Brother's Day cards, the recipe for the punch, and a sign I had made. The sign said (what else?): HAPPY BROTHER'S DAY!

I found my presents and put them into a grocery bag.

"Which is mine? What's in it?" cried Andrew. He was hopping around. He was

70

gigundo excited. "Why did you have to wrap them up?" he asked.

"Because they're surprises," I replied.

"I want to know what mine is!"

"Andrew, this is like your birthday. Or like Christmas," I explained. "You have to wait until the right time to open presents."

"Okay! Okay!" Andrew was still hopping around.

I gathered up my cards and the recipe and the sign.

"Uh-oh," I said. I rummaged around in my stuff. I pulled out Seth's present. Then I pulled out the cards for Seth and Midgie. "Mommy, are you *sure* Seth and Midgie can't come to the party?"

"Honey, I've already told you," Mommy replied. "Seth will be out of town tomorrow. He has to go on a business trip."

"I know. But what about Midgie?"

"Karen, I am not going to drive a dog to a party," said Mommy. "That's silly."

"But Midgie might have fun."

"No." Mommy shook her head.

I sighed. "All right. Will you be *sure* to give Midgie his card tomorrow? And to give Seth his card and present before he leaves?"

"I promise," said Mommy.

"Thank you," I replied.

I looked at my stuff. I hoped I had not forgotten anything important. Because ready or not, I had to give a Brother's Day party the next day.

I decided I was ready.

"Mommy, is it time to go to Daddy's yet?"

"Not yet." Mommy sounded tired.

"Are you sure we can't go early?"

"I'm sure."

"Okay." I rehearsed the apology speech I was going to make. I said it until Mommy finally called, "Time to go to Daddy's!"

"Hurray!" I cried.

And Andrew said, "I can't *wait* for Brother's Day!"

16

Happy Brother's Day

"Happy Brother's Day!" I shouted.

It was Saturday. I was in the playroom at the big house. On the table was the box of chocolate chip (and plain) cookies. Next to the cookies was the punch. Next to the punch was the stack of Brother's Day cards. And next to the cards were the presents. I was standing in the doorway. The first guests were arriving. They were Andrew, David Michael, and Sam. Next came Charlie and Daddy, who was holding Boo-Boo. (Boo-Boo did not seem to want to come to

73

the party. I had to close the door to keep him in the playroom.)

Just as I was closing the door, I heard *knock, knock.*

I opened the door. There stood Ricky!

"You *did* come!" I cried. "Happy Brother's Day! Hurry inside before Boo-Boo gets loose."

Ricky squeezed into the playroom.

When all the guests were sitting down, I said, "Happy Brother's Day! This is the first Brother's Day party ever. I hope there will be more."

Sam and Charlie smiled. They were on their best behavior. Daddy must have talked to them earlier in the morning.

"Okay," I went on. "Time for the party to start. First we should eat."

"Good," said Charlie. "I'm hungry."

I passed around the box of cookies. Then I served punch to everyone.

"Yum," said David Michael. "Thank you, Karen."

"Yeah, thanks," mumbled Ricky.

When we had eaten the refreshments, I recited my apology speech. "Dads, friends, pets, and especially brothers," I began. I waited for someone to snicker. No one did. "I want to say that I know I have not been nice to you lately. I thought I hated all boys. But I was wrong. And so I'm — I'm — "

"Go ahead. Say it," said Sam. (I bet he thought I couldn't.)

So I said loudly and clearly, "I am very, very sorry. Now, let's have some more fun. It's time for games!"

"Games," repeated Andrew. "I want to open the presents and cards."

I almost said, "No, Andrew. Don't be a baby." But it was Brother's Day. So instead I said, "All right."

First I handed out the cards. I had made very sweet cards. Andrew's said: FOR A DEAR BROTHER ON BROTHER'S DAY. The others said things like that, too. Except for Ricky's. Ricky's said: HAPPY

BROTHER'S DAY TO MY BELOVED HUS-
BAND. (It had more glitter than anyone
else's.)

Ricky smiled at me. I felt gigundo relieved.

"*Now* open the presents!" exclaimed
Andrew.

"Okay, okay." I passed out the presents.
Everyone tore off the wrapping paper. I had
made a drum for Andrew and also for David
Michael. I had made pencil cups for Daddy,
Charlie, and Sam. But Ricky's present was
different. It was special. I had made him a
piggy bank.

"Gosh, thanks, Karen," said Ricky.

"How about games now?" I suggested.

But just then David Michael said, "Uh-
oh!" and jumped up. He grabbed Boo-Boo.
"Boo-Boo was trying to figure out how to
catch the goldfish!" he cried. He carried
Boo-Boo to the door. He put him in the
hallway.

Then Charlie said, "Karen, I'm really
sorry, but I have to go."

"Me, too," said Sam. "This was a great party, Karen. We should celebrate Brother's Day every year!"

"And maybe next year, we will celebrate Sister's Day, too," added Daddy.

17

Karen and Ricky Again

The Brother's Day party was over. Everyone had left the room. Except for Ricky and Goldfishie and me. I could hear Andrew banging away on his drum.

I looked around the playroom. "I have to clean up this mess," I said to Ricky.

"I'll help you," he offered. "I don't have to go home right away."

"Thanks, Ricky."

Ricky and I collected the wrapping paper and envelopes and napkins in a big bag. We wiped up cookie crumbs and punch spills.

When the playroom looked clean again, I said to Ricky, "Want to go outdoors for awhile?"

"Okay."

Ricky and I went into the backyard. At first I was afraid we would not know what to say to each other. It had been a long time since our fight had begun. But Ricky spoke up. He said, "Karen, how come you stopped talking to me?"

I blushed. "Because . . . because, um, well, I know this sounds funny, but I was jealous of Bobby Gianelli."

"Bobby?! Why?" Ricky wanted to know.

"Because you were spending so much time with him. And when the two of you got together to play football, you said I couldn't play. You said I was a girl."

"You *are* a girl," Ricky pointed out.

"I know. But I can still play football. Besides, I'm your friend — and your wife," I reminded Ricky. "I felt left out. I felt ignored."

"Is that why *you* ignored *me*?"

80

"I guess so," I replied. "I know I wasn't being nice."

"That's okay. I'm sorry you thought I ignored you. But I *do* like to play with Bobby. He's good at football."

"Well, so am I," I said. "Watch this."

I ran into the garage, found an old football, and passed it to Ricky.

"Hey, you *are* good!" he exclaimed. "Can you catch?"

"Yup. Throw the ball back to me."

Ricky did so, and when I caught it, I clutched it with two hands. I held it against my chest like Sam had taught me to do. "I can run fast, too," I told Ricky.

"Wow. . . . Would you like to play ball with Bobby and me and some other kids on Monday? I'd really like you to."

"You *would? Sure!*"

Ricky's mother arrived then, so Ricky had to go home.

The rest of the big-house weekend was nice — except that Andrew would not stop beating on his drum.

18

"Bet You Can't!"

"Hi, Karen!"

"Hi, Ricky!"

It was Monday morning. Another week of school was starting. My classmates and I were gathering in Ms. Colman's room.

Everyone could see that Ricky and I were friends again. Most of the kids did not say anything about it. Pamela did not, ei- ther — at first. She just sat at her desk and frowned. I noticed that she and Jannie and Leslie were still wearing their "I ♥ Boys" buttons.

I sat at my desk in the front row. Ricky sat next to me at his desk.

"You know what?" he said. "I put all my money in the bank you made for me. I have almost ten dollars. I found forty-five cents under my parents' bed, and Dad said I could keep it."

"What are you saving up for?" I asked loudly. I had realized that Pamela was listening to Ricky and me. I wanted to be sure she caught every word.

"Something secret," Ricky answered. He was smiling.

"For me?" I asked.

"Maybe."

I knew that meant yes, so I said, "Thank you, Ricky!"

That was too much for Pamela. She marched over to Ricky and me. "In case you have forgotten, Karen," she said, "you are not speaking to Ricky. Neither is anyone else in your stupid boy-hating club." I started to say something, but Pamela would not let me. "It is so babyish to hate boys," she went on. "Cool girls *like* boys." (I tried to remind Pamela that I was married to Ricky. She would not listen.) "I've seen your club sign. You think it's a secret. Well, it isn't." Pamela held her two fingers out in front of her, but they made a T sign.

"For your information, Pamela Harding," I began, "that sign is *wrong*. This is the right sign." (I made the X.) "And it is not a secret. Plus, there is no more We Hate Boys Club. Is there?" I demanded. I turned to Nancy and Hannie.

They crossed their arms and shook their heads. They held their noses in the air.

"Nope. No more club," said Nancy.

"And anyway, you did not even know about our other sign," added Hannie.

"What other sign?" asked Pamela. She was not shouting anymore.

"This one," Hannie replied. She went to the chalkboard. She drew:

Pamela's face grew red. A couple of kids snickered.

I saw that Leslie and Jannie had taken off their buttons.

Pamela looked from her friends to my friends and me.

"Ricky and I are not mad at each other anymore," I told Pamela.

"You aren't?"

"Nope. In fact, I am going to play football with the boys at recess today."

"*Really?*" Pamela looked confused. Upset, too.

"Ricky asked me to," I told Pamela. "And since you like boys so much — since it is cool to like boys — why don't you play with

us? I dare you to play on the other team.
Ricky and I will beat you guys."

"We-ell," said Pamela.

"I bet you can't even play football," I said.

"Bet I can." Pamela did not sound very
sure of herself.

"Bet you can't."

"Can too!"

"Great. See you on the football field!"

"*O-kay!*" yelled Pamela.

19

"No Fair!"

The morning crawled by. I like school. But on that Monday, I was only looking forward to recess. And football.

Finally the morning ended. Lunch ended. Ricky, Bobby, seven other boys, and I met on the football field. Hannie, Nancy, Natalie, and a bunch of second-graders followed us. They were going to watch the game. They wanted to see Ricky and me and our team beat Pamela and the other team.

But someone important was missing.

"Where's Pamela?" asked Nancy.

Pamela had not joined us.

"She better play," I said. "She *bet* she could. I dared her to." I looked around the playground. "Hey, there she is!"

Pamela, Leslie, and Jannie were huddled in a far corner of the playground.

"She's not going to play," said Bobby.

"Oh, yes she is!" I replied. "Hey, Pamela! Come here!"

Pamela turned around slowly.

"COME . . . HERE!" I yelled. "Everyone is waiting for you."

Pamela dragged herself across the playground. Her friends followed her.

"See? She's coming after all," I announced.

But when Pamela reached us, she said, "No fair. I can't play. I'm wearing a dress. Everyone else is wearing pants."

"Okay. Wear pants tomorrow. Play with us then," I said. I smiled.

Pamela looked trapped. She would have to play football one way or the other.

"No," she said after a moment. "I'll play

now. I might as well get it over with."

"Good," I replied. "Before we start the game, let's show the boys what we can do. Let's show them how we can throw the ball and catch it. You run over there," I told Pamela. I pointed to a place ahead of me.

Pamela walked to the spot. She held out her arms. "Okay, I'm ready."

I threw the ball toward Pamela. It was a good pass. Pamela missed it by a mile.

"Gee, that was great," I told her.

Pamela made a face at me. Then she picked up the football. She threw it back to me. Only she wound up and threw it like a baseball.

Even so, I managed to catch it.

Pamela smiled at Ricky. Then she pouted. "Ricky, I — "

But Ricky interrupted her. "Pamela, Karen. Are you going to play with us or not?"

"Yeah," said Bobby crossly. "Let's get going. We're wasting time."

"What about my dress?" asked Pamela.

Ricky took the football away from me. "This is stupid," he said. "I don't care who plays or who doesn't play today."

"As long as we play," asked Bobby. "Recess is half over. Come *on*."

By that time, an even bigger crowd was watching us. All of the kids in both second-grade classrooms were standing around.

"Well, *I'm* ready to play!" I said.

"Good," replied Ricky. "Come on, Karen. Pamela, you don't have to play."

Pamela's face fell. Her eyes filled with tears. "Ricky?" she said.

"Listen," he answered gently. "I like you as a friend, Pamela. But Karen is my wife." Ricky put his arm across my shoulders.

Most of the kids began to snicker. But I hardly noticed. I was thinking. So Ricky *did* like Pamela. But I was *special* to him. That was gigundo important.

Pamela turned her back. She walked away.

"Okay!" cried Bobby. "Let's go!"

20

"Home Run!"

I watched Pamela. She walked slowly across the playground. Leslie and Jannie went with her. I felt sort of sorry for the We ♥ Boys Club. But I did not feel sorry enough to apologize to them.

Anyway, the game was about to start. I ran around just like I do with my brothers. Sometimes I made mistakes. But I also caught some passes. I almost scored a touchdown!

"Hey, Ricky! Karen! Can I play, too?"

Nancy was calling to us from the crowd.

Ricky looked at Bobby. Then he looked at me. He shrugged. "Why not?" he said.

"Sure you can play, Nancy!" I called to her.

As soon as Nancy ran onto the field, about ten more kids asked if *they* could play. I guess because we looked like we were having fun.

Ricky and Bobby did not say no to anyone. Even to Natalie. (Natalie is a klutz. Also a crier.) Soon, so many kids wanted to play that we almost had enough people to make three teams. We just made two huge teams, though.

We ran and kicked the ball and tossed it. Everyone was laughing.

Do you know what? We could not even tell who was on which team. When Nancy caught the ball and ran all the way to the end of the field, she yelled, "I did it!" But nobody knew what side she had scored for.

We did not care.

We did not care when Hank Reubens threw the ball into the woods and we had to search for it.

We did not care when the twins switched sides without telling anyone.

We did not care when Bobby scored a touchdown and Natalie yelled, "Home run!"

But we did care when the bell rang. Recess was over.

"Ohhh . . . " we groaned.

"I can't believe it," said Nancy.

"Recess went too fast," I added.

"Let's all play again tomorrow," suggested Ricky.

"*Really?*" cried Natalie.

"Yeah. This was fun, wasn't it?" said Bobby.

"It was great!" I exclaimed.

Everyone began to walk back to school. In front of me, Nancy was walking with Bobby. Bobby was saying to her, "No, a *half*back is . . . "

I smiled to myself. I was happy to see

that Nancy and Bobby were together.

I was even happier that Ricky and I were together again, though. I looked at my husband. "I'm glad we're friends," I told him. "I'm glad we're married."

"Me, too." Ricky was holding the football in one arm. He slipped his other arm through mine. We kept on walking.

"Ricky?" I said.

"Yeah?"

"Let's not fight anymore, okay?"

"Well, let's *try* not to fight anymore," said Ricky. "Sometimes people *need* to fight."

"Right," I agreed. "But let's try *very* hard not to fight. I don't like being mad at you."

"And I don't like being mad at you."

"Will we be husband and wife forever?" I asked Ricky. (I did not really mean forever. I just meant until the end of second grade.)

"We'll be husband and wife at least until Natalie learns to play football," Ricky replied. He was grinning.

I grinned back. I did not have a thing to worry about.

About the Author

ANN M. MARTIN lives in New York City and loves animals. Her cat, Mouse, knows how to take the phone off the hook.

Other books by Ann M. Martin that you might enjoy are *Stage Fright*, *Me and Katie (the Pest)*, and the books in *The Baby-sitters Club* series.

Ann likes ice cream, the beach, and *I Love Lucy*. And she has her own little sister, whose name is Jane.

Little Sister

Don't miss #18

KAREN'S HOME RUN

David Michael wound up and pitched the ball.

I kept my eyes on it. When the time seemed right, I swung the bat. Hard.

WHACK! I hit the ball! I could not even see where it went. That was how fast it was flying. "Boy . . ." I said softly.

"Run, Karen!" Kristy cried.

I ran. I touched first base, second base, third base, and finally I was running across home plate.

"Home run!" shouted Kristy.

Everyone began to cheer for me. I had hit the ball *so* hard that we could not even find it.

Now, I thought, I will *really* be happy to march in the parade with the Krushers. Maybe my teammates would even start calling me Home Run Karen or something.

You Can Be the Lucky BIRTHDAY KID!

Join the

BABY·SITTERS ™

Little Sister

Birthday Club!

Happy Birthday to you! Join the **Baby-sitters Little Sister Birthday Club** and on your birthday, you'll receive a personalized card from Karen herself!

That's not all! Every month, a **BIRTHDAY KID OF THE MONTH** will be randomly chosen to **WIN** a complete set of *Baby-sitters Little Sister* books! The set's first book will be autographed by author Ann M. Martin!

Just fill in the coupon below. Offer expires March 31, 1992. Fill in the coupon below or write the information on a 3" x 5" piece of paper and mail to: BABY-SITTERS LITTLE SISTER BIRTHDAY CLUB, Scholastic Inc., 730 Broadway, P.O. Box 742, New York, New York 10003.

Baby-sitters Little Sister Birthday Club

❏ **YES!** I want to join the BABY-SITTERS LITTLE SISTER BIRTHDAY CLUB!

My birthday is _____

Name _____ Age _____

Street _____

City _____ State _____ Zip _____

P.S. Please put your birthday on the outside of your envelope too! Thanks!

Where did you buy this *Baby-sitters Little Sister* book?

❏ Bookstore ❏ Drugstore ❏ Supermarket ❏ Library
❏ Book Club ❏ Book Fair ❏ Other_____(specify)

Available in U.S. and Canada only.   BLS890

Kristy is Karen's older stepsister, and she and her friends are...

THE BABY-SITTERS CLUB®

by Ann M. Martin, author of *Baby-sitters Little Sister*™